For my mother, with all my heart – H.W.

For Anni, Samu and Sara – A.S.

Text copyright © 2002 by Anu Stohner
Illustrations copyright © 2002 by Henrike Wilson
Translation copyright © 2004 by Anna Trenter
Translated from the original German by Anna Trenter
First published in Germany 2002 by Carl Hanser Verlag

Published by Bloomsbury, New York and London
Distributed to the trade by Holtzbrinck Publishers

Library of Congress Cataloging-in-Publication Data
available upon request
ISBN 1-58234-964-9

First U.S. Edition 2004
Printed & bound in China by South China Printing Co
3 5 7 9 10 8 6 4

Bloomsbury USA Children's Books
175 Fifth Avenue
New York, NY 10010

All papers used by Bloomsbury Publishing are natural, recyclable products made from wood
grown in well-managed forests. The manufacturing processes conform to the
environmental regulations of the country of origin.

Santa's Littlest Helper

by Anu Stohner

illustrated by Henrike Wilson

BLOOMSBURY
CHILDREN'S
BOOKS

Far, far in the North, where the first snow falls in summertime,
a special village is hidden away – the village where Santa and all
his Helpers live. And in that village lived a little Helper who couldn't
wait for Christmas.

He was always the first to bring a Christmas tree back from the great forest, the first to clean his sleigh, polish his boots and spruce up his red Christmas coat.

As for presents, the littlest Helper had his wrapped and ready while the other Helpers were still choosing theirs.
He liked to give toys that he had made himself. He could make all sorts of things, like brightly colored cars, spotted wooden dogs, rocking horses and dollhouses.

He also baked wonderful cinnamon stars, honey cakes and chocolate cookies. His gingerbread was the finest in the whole world.

Once all the presents were wrapped and cookies baked, he
looked forward to delivering them to the children. But every
year the same thing happened . . .

"No, you can't come," said the Chief Helper, who was in charge of everything in the village. "You are too small."

"The children would laugh their heads off!" shouted one Helper.

"If they could even see him," laughed another.

"With his tiny sleigh!" said a third.

The Chief Helper just smiled and said to the littlest Helper, "Perhaps next year." But the littlest Helper was beginning to doubt it.

He didn't want to see or hear the other Helpers set off on their journey with Santa, so he closed the shutters and stayed in his room all alone. He didn't mind that he was smaller than the others, but he was very sad that he wasn't allowed to go and visit the children.

In the evening, when everything lay quiet and deserted, he ventured outside. He wasn't allowed to fly with the others, but he could at least stretch his legs. The stars twinkled, but the little Helper didn't look at them. The others would be flying up there somewhere in their reindeer sleigh . . . Then suddenly he heard voices in the great forest. Only the animals lived in the forest. What were they talking about so late at night?

The littlest Helper was
small enough to sneak up close
without the animals noticing him.
The squirrel was there, and the hare,
the bear, the wild pig and the mice . . .
They were all complaining.

"It's not fair," growled the bear. "Santa and his Helpers take
presents to humans every year, but they never come to us animals."

"And we're right on their doorstep," grumbled the hare.

"It's always been like that," sighed the old owl. "I'm afraid it will
never change."

But it did change! As soon as the little Helper heard what the animals were saying, he silently slipped away and ran home. He checked his clothes in the mirror, packed the presents onto his sleigh, and then he was off again. He had no reindeer, as they had all gone with the other Helpers, but he could easily push the sleigh as far as the forest.

That evening the animals had a party. The great forest had never seen anything like it. All the animals received presents, but the growly bear was happiest of all – he had never been given anything in his life before. And the owl was proudest – she tried on her new pullover and was instantly the best-dressed bird in the whole forest.

As soon as the other Helpers returned, the littlest Helper went to the Chief and told him what had happened. The Chief Helper was amazed and named him "Santa for the Animals."

"Bravo!" shouted the others, and they carried him high on their shoulders. And ever since then, the littlest Helper has been just as important as the big ones.

Every

single

year.